# Pip Sits

## MARY MORGAN

I Like to Read®

Holiday House / New York

Copyright © 2017 by Mary Vanroyen
All Rights Reserved
HOLIDAY HOUSE is registered in the U.S. Patent and Trademark Office.
Printed and Bound in November 2016 at Tien Wah Press, Johor Bahru, Johor, Malaysia.
The artwork was created with watercolor, gouache and colored pencil.
www.holidayhouse.com
First Edition
1 3 5 7 9 10 8 6 4 2

Library of Congress Cataloging-in-Publication Data
Names: Morgan, Mary, author.
Title: Pip sits / Mary Morgan.
Description: First edition. | New York : Holiday House, [2017] | Series: I
like to read | Summary: Pip the porcupine sits on a nest of eggs, and when
they hatch, the chicks think Pip is their mother.
Identifiers: LCCN 2016004118 | ISBN 9780823436767 (hardcover)
Subjects: | CYAC: Porcupines—Fiction. | Ducks—Fiction. |
Animals—Infancy—Fiction. | Mother and child—Fiction.
Classification: LCC PZ7.M82533 Pi 2017 | DDC [E]—dc23 LC record available at https://lccn.loc.gov/2016004118

ISBN 978-0-8234-3778-8 (paperback)

For Olivia Rose and Mirabelle Grace

Mom sits.
Pip looks for fun.

Pip goes up.

He jumps.

He plops.

He peeks.

Pip sees Mother Duck.
"I have to go,"
says Mother Duck.
"Will you sit
on my eggs?"

Pip gets
in the nest.

Pip sits.

He hears
a tap.

He feels
a poke.

A duck comes out.

Mama!

"Mama!" it says.

Pop!

Pop!

Pop!

Pop!

All the ducks
come out.
"Mama!"
they say.

Mama

Mama

Mama

Pip loves
the ducks.
They sit.

They sleep.

Peep          Peep

One peeps.

They all peep.

Peep

Peep

Peep

Peep

Peep

Peep

Peep

Peep

The ducks want to eat.

Mother Duck comes.

My babies!

Peep

Peep

But the babies want Pip.

"Come!" says Mother Duck.
"Come!" says Pip.

Quack!

The ducks like water.

Plop

Flop

Pip does not.

Pip cries.
His mother comes.

Everyone is happy!